HORRID HENRY's
Teacher Torture

Francesca Simon spent her childhood on the beach
in California, and then went to Yale and Oxford
Universities to study medieval history and literature.
She now lives in London with her family. She has
written over 45 books and won the Children's Book
of the Year in 2008 at the Galaxy British Book Awards
for *Horrid Henry and the Abominable Snowman*.

HORRID HENRY'S
Teacher Torture

Francesca Simon
Illustrated by Tony Ross

Orion
Children's Books

Horrid Henry's New Teacher originally appeared in *Horrid Henry Tricks the Tooth Fairy* first published in Great Britain in 1996
Horrid Henry's School Trip originally appeared in *Horrid Henry's Nits* first published in Great Britain in 1997
Horrid Henry and the Demon Dinner Lady originally appeared in *Horrid Henry's Revenge* first published in Great Britain in 2001
Horrid Henry's Sports Day originally appeared in *Horrid Henry Gets Rich Quick* first published in Great Britain in 1998
This edition first published in Great Britain in 2009
by Orion Children's Books
a division of the Orion Publishing Group Ltd
Orion House
5 Upper Saint Martin's Lane
London WC2H 9EA
An Hachette UK Company

1 3 5 7 9 10 8 6 4 2

Text © Francesca Simon 1996, 1997, 1998, 2001
Illustrations © Tony Ross 1996, 1997, 1998, 2001

ISBN: 978 1 44400 047 4

A catalogue record for this book is available from the British Library.

Printed in Great Britain by Clays Ltd, St Ives plc

www.horridhenry.co.uk
www.orionbooks.co.uk

CONTENTS

HORRID HENRY'S NEW TEACHER

"Now Henry," said Dad. "Today is the first day of school. A chance for a fresh start with a new teacher."

"Yeah, yeah," scowled Horrid Henry.

He hated the first day of term. Another year, another teacher to show who was boss. His first teacher, Miss Marvel, had run screaming from the classroom after two weeks. His next teacher, Mrs Zip, had run screaming from the classroom after one day. Breaking in new teachers wasn't easy, thought Henry, but someone had to do it.

Dad got out a piece of paper and waved it.

"Henry, I never want to read another school report like this again," he said. "Why can't your school reports be like Peter's?"

Henry started whistling.

"Pay attention, Henry," shouted Dad. "This is important. Look at this report."

HENRY'S SCHOOL REPORT

It has been horrible Teaching Henry this year. He is rude, lazy and disruptive. The worst student I have ever taught.

Behaviour: Horrid

English: Horrid

Maths: Horrid

Science: Horrid

P.E: Horrid

"What about *my* report?" said Perfect Peter.

Dad beamed.

"Your report was perfect, Peter," said Dad. "Keep up the wonderful work."

PETER'S SCHOOL REPORT

It has been a pleasure teaching Peter this year. He is polite, hard-working and co-operative. The best student I have ever taught.

Behaviour: Perfect

English: Perfect

Maths: Perfect

Science: Perfect

P.E: Perfect

Peter smiled proudly.

"You'll just have to try harder, Henry," said Peter, smirking.

Horrid Henry was a shark sinking his teeth into a drowning sailor.

"OWWWW," shrieked Peter. "Henry bit me!"

"Don't be horrid, Henry!" shouted Dad. "Or no TV for a week."

"I don't care," muttered Henry. When he became King he'd make it a law that parents, not children, had to go to school.

Horrid Henry pushed and shoved his way into class and grabbed the seat next to Rude Ralph.

"Nah nah ne nah nah, I've got a new football," said Ralph.

Henry didn't have a football. He'd kicked his through Moody Margaret's window.

"Who cares?" said Horrid Henry.

The classroom door slammed. It was

Mr Nerdon, the toughest, meanest, nastiest teacher in the school.

"SILENCE!" he said, glaring at them with his bulging eyes. "I don't want to hear a sound. I don't even want to hear anyone breathe."

The class held its breath.

"GOOD!" he growled. "I'm Mr Nerdon."

Henry snorted. What a stupid name.

"Nerd," he whispered to Ralph.

Rude Ralph giggled.

"Nerdy Nerd," whispered Horrid Henry, snickering.

Mr Nerdon walked up to Henry and jabbed his finger in his face.

"Quiet, you horrible boy!" said Mr Nerdon. "I've got my eye on you. Oh yes. I've heard about your other teachers. Bah! I'm made of stronger stuff. There will be no nonsense in *my* class."

We'll see about that, thought Henry.

"Our first sums for the year are on the board. Now get to work," ordered Mr Nerdon.

Horrid Henry had an idea.

Quickly he scribbled a note to Ralph.

Ralph - I bet you that I can Make Mr. Nerdon run screaming out of class by the end of lunchtime.

No way, Henry
If I do will you give me your new football?

O.K. But if you don't, you have to give me your pound coin.

O.K.

Horrid Henry took a deep breath and went to work. He rolled up some paper, stuffed it in his mouth, and spat it out. The spitball whizzed through the air and pinged Mr Nerdon on the back of his neck.

Mr Nerdon wheeled round.

"You!" snapped Mr Nerdon. "Don't you mess with me!"

"It wasn't *me*!" said Henry. "It was Ralph."

"Liar!" said Mr Nerdon. "Sit at the back of the class."

Horrid Henry moved his seat next to Clever Clare.

"Move over, Henry!" hissed Clare. "You're on my side of the desk."

Henry shoved her.

"Move over yourself," he hissed back.

Then Horrid Henry reached over and broke Clare's pencil.

"Henry broke my pencil!" shrieked Clare.

Mr Nerdon moved Henry next to Weepy William.

Henry pinched him.

Mr Nerdon moved Henry next to Tough Toby.

Henry jiggled the desk.

Mr Nerdon moved Henry next to Lazy Linda.

Henry scribbled all over her paper.

Mr Nerdon moved Henry next to Moody Margaret.

Moody Margaret drew a line down the middle of the desk.

"Cross that line, Henry, and you're dead," said Margaret under her breath.

Henry looked up. Mr Nerdon was writing spelling words on the board.

Henry started to rub out Margaret's line.

"Stop it, Henry," said Mr Nerdon, without turning round.

Henry stopped.

Mr Nerdon continued writing.

Henry pulled Margaret's hair.

Mr Nerdon moved Henry next to Beefy Bert, the biggest boy in the class.

Beefy Bert was chewing his pencil and trying to add 2 + 2 without much luck.

Horrid Henry inched his chair on to Beefy Bert's side of the desk.

Bert ignored him.

Henry poked him.

Bert ignored him.

Henry hit him.

POW!

The next thing Henry knew he was lying on the floor, looking up at the ceiling. Beefy Bert continued chewing his pencil.

"What happened, Bert?" said Mr Nerdon.

"I dunno," said Beefy Bert.

"Get up off the floor, Henry!" said Mr Nerdon. A faint smile appeared on the teacher's slimy lips.

"He hit me!" said Henry. He'd never

felt such a punch in his life.

"It was an accident," said Mr Nerdon. He smirked. "You'll sit next to Bert from now on."

That's it, thought Henry. Now it's war.

"How absurd, to be a nerdy bird," said Horrid Henry behind Mr Nerdon's back.

Slowly Mr Nerdon turned and walked towards him. His hand was clenched into a fist.

"Since you're so good at rhyming," said Mr Nerdon. "Everyone write a poem. Now."

Henry slumped in his seat and groaned. A poem! Yuck! He hated poems. Even the word *poem* made him want to throw up.

Horrid Henry caught Rude Ralph's eye. Ralph was grinning and mouthing, "A pound, a pound!" at him. Time was running out. Despite Henry's best efforts, Mr Nerdon still hadn't run screaming from the class. Henry would have to act fast to get that football.

What horrible poem could he write? Horrid Henry smiled. Quickly he picked up his pencil and went to work.

"Now, who's my first victim?" said Mr Nerdon. He looked round the room. "Susan! Read your poem."

Sour Susan stood up and read:

"Bow wow
Bow wow
Woof woof woof
I'm a dog, not a cat, so . . .
SCAT!"

"Not enough rhymes," said Mr

Nerdon. "Next . . ." He looked round the room. "Graham!"

Greedy Graham stood up and read:

"Chocolate chocolate chocolate sweet,
  Cakes and doughnuts can't be beat.
    Ice cream is my favourite treat
    With lots and lots of pie to eat!"

"Too many rhymes," said Mr Nerdon. "Next . . ." He scowled at the class. Henry tried to look as if he didn't want the teacher to call on him.

"Henry!" snapped Mr Nerdon. "Read your poem!"

Horrid Henry stood up and read:

"Pirates puke on stormy seas,
  Giants spew on top of trees."

Henry peeked at Mr Nerdon. He
looked pale. Henry continued to read:

"Kings are sick in golden loos,
    Dogs throw up on Daddy's shoes."

Henry peeked again at Mr Nerdon. He
looked green. Any minute now, thought
Henry, and he'll be out of here
screaming. He read on:

"Babies love to make a mess,
    Down the front of Mum's best dress.

And what car ride would be complete,
Without the stink of last night's treat?"

"That's enough," choked Mr Nerdon.

"Wait, I haven't got to the good bit," said Horrid Henry.

"I said that's enough!" gasped Mr Nerdon. "You fail."

He made a big black mark in his book.

"I threw up on the boat!" shouted Greedy Graham.

"I threw up on the plane!" shouted Sour Susan.

"I threw up in the car!" shouted Dizzy Dave.

"I said that's enough!" ordered Mr Nerdon. He glared at Horrid Henry. "Get out of here, all of you! It's lunchtime."

Rats, thought Henry. Mr Nerdon was one tough teacher.

Rude Ralph grabbed him.

"Ha ha, Henry," said Ralph. "You lose. Gimme that pound."

"No," said Henry. "I've got until the end of lunch."

"You can't do anything to him between now and then," said Ralph.

"Oh yeah?" said Henry. "Just watch me."

Then Henry had a wonderful, spectacular idea. This was it. The best plan he'd ever had. Someday someone would stick a plaque on the school wall celebrating Henry's genius. There would be songs written about him. He'd probably even get a medal. But first things first. In order for his plan to work to perfection, he needed Peter.

Perfect Peter was playing hopscotch with his friends Tidy Ted and Spotless Sam.

"Hey Peter," said Henry. "How would you like to be a real member of the Purple Hand?"

The Purple Hand was Horrid Henry's secret club. Peter had wanted to join for ages, but naturally Henry would never let him.

Peter's jaw dropped open.

"Me?" said Peter.

"Yes," said Henry. "If you can pass the secret club test."

"What do I have to do?" said Peter eagerly.

"It's tricky," said Henry. "And probably much too hard for you."

"Tell me, tell me," said Peter.

"All you have to do is lie down right there below that window and stay absolutely still. You mustn't move until I tell you to."

"Why?" said Peter.

"Because that's the test," said Henry.

Perfect Peter thought for a moment.

"Are you going to drop something on me?"

"No," said Henry.

"OK," said Peter. He lay down obediently.

"And I need your shoes," said Henry.

"Why?" said Peter.

Henry scowled.

"Do you want to be in the Purple Hand or not?" said Henry.

"I do," said Peter.

"Then give me your shoes and be quiet," said Henry. "I'll be checking on you. If I see you moving one little bit you can't be in my club."

Peter gave Henry his trainers, then lay still as a statue.

Horrid Henry grabbed the shoes, then dashed up the stairs to his classroom.

It was empty. Good.

Horrid Henry went over to the window and opened it. Then he stood there, holding one of Peter's shoes in each hand.

Henry waited until he heard Mr Nerdon's footsteps. Then he went into action.

"Help!" shouted Horrid Henry. "Help!"

Mr Nerdon entered. He saw Henry and glowered.

"What are you doing here? Get out!"

"Help!" shouted Henry. "I can't hold on to him much longer . . . he's slipping . . . aaahhh, he's fallen!"

Horrid Henry held up the empty shoes.

"He's gone," whispered Henry. He peeked out of the window. "Ugghh, I can't look."

Mr Nerdon went pale. He ran to the window and saw Perfect Peter lying still and shoeless on the ground below.

"Oh no," gasped Mr Nerdon.

"I'm sorry," panted Henry. "I tried to hold on to him, honest, I – "

"Help!" screamed Mr Nerdon. He raced down the stairs. "Police! Fire! Ambulance! Help! Help!"

He ran over to Peter and knelt by his still body.

"Can I get up now, Henry?" said Perfect Peter.

"What!?" gasped Mr Nerdon. "What did you say?"

Then the terrible truth dawned. He, Ninius Nerdon, had been tricked.

"YOU HORRID BOY! GO STRAIGHT TO THE HEAD TEACHER – NOW!" screeched Mr Nerdon.

Perfect Peter jumped to his feet.

"But . . . but –" spluttered Perfect Peter.

"Now!" screamed Mr Nerdon. "How dare you! To the head!"

"AAAGGGHHHH," shrieked Peter.

He slunk off to the head's office, weeping.

Mr Nerdon turned to race up the stairs to grab Henry.

"I'll get you, Henry!" he screamed. His face was white. He looked as if he were going to faint.

"Help," squeaked Mr Nerdon.

Then he fainted.

Clunk! Thunk! Thud!

NEE NAW NEE NAW NEE NAW.

When the ambulance arrived, the only person lying on the ground was Mr Nerdon. They scooped him on to a stretcher and took him away.

The perfect end to a perfect day, thought Horrid Henry, throwing his new football in the air. Peter sent home in disgrace. Mr Nerdon gone for good. Even the news that scary Miss Battle-Axe would be teaching Henry's class didn't bother him. After all, tomorrow was another day.

2

HORRID HENRY'S SCHOOL TRIP

"Don't forget my packed lunch for the school trip," shouted Horrid Henry for the tenth time. "I want crisps, biscuits, chocolate, and a fizzywizz drink."

"No way, Henry," said Dad grimly, slicing carrots. "I'm making you a healthy, nutritious lunch."

"But I don't want a healthy lunch," howled Henry. "I like sweets!"

"Sweets, yuck," said Perfect Peter.

He peeked in his lunch box.

"Oh boy, an apple!" said Peter. "And egg and cress on brown bread with the crusts on! And carrot and celery sticks, my favourite! Thank you so much, Dad. Henry, if you don't eat healthy food, you'll never grow big and strong."

"Oh yeah," said Henry. "I'll show you how big and strong I am, you little pipsqueak," he added, springing at Peter. He was a boa constrictor throttling his prey.

"Uggghhhh," choked Peter.

"Stop being horrid, Henry!" shouted Mum. "Or there will be no school trip for you."

Henry let Peter go. Horrid Henry loved school trips. No work. No assembly. A packed lunch. A chance to fool around all day. What could be better?

"I'm going to the Frosty Freeze Ice Cream factory," said Henry. "Free ice creams for everyone. Yippee!"

Perfect Peter made a face. "I don't like ice cream," he said. "My class is going somewhere much better – our Town Museum. And Mum's coming to help."

"I'd rather be boiled alive and eaten by cannibals than go to that boring old dump," said Horrid Henry, shuddering. Mum had dragged him there once. Never again.

Then Henry noticed Peter's T-shirt. It was exactly the same as his, purple striped with gold stars.

"Tell Peter to stop copying what I wear to school!" screamed Henry.

"It doesn't matter, Henry," said Mum. "You're going on different trips. No one will notice."

"Just keep out of my way, Peter," snarled Henry. "I don't want anyone to think we're related."

Horrid Henry's class buzzed with excitement as they scrambled to be first on the bus.

"I've got crisps!" shouted Dizzy Dave.

"I've got biscuits!" shouted Anxious Andrew.

"I've got toffee and chocolate and lollies and three fizzywizzes!" shouted Greedy Graham.

"WAAAA," wailed Weepy
William. "I forgot my packed lunch."

"Quiet!" ordered Miss Battle-Axe
as the bus started moving. "Sit still
and behave. No eating on the bus.
William, stop weeping."

"I need a wee!" shouted Lazy Linda.

"Well, you'll have to wait,"
snapped Miss Battle-Axe.

Horrid Henry had trampled his
way to the window seats at the back
next to Rude Ralph and Greedy
Graham. He liked those seats best.
Miss Battle-Axe couldn't see him, and
he could make faces at all the people
in the cars behind him.

Henry and Ralph rolled down the
window and chanted:

"Beans, beans, good for the heart,
The more you eat, the more you –"
"HENRY!" bellowed Miss

Battle-Axe. "Turn around and face forward NOW!"

"I need a wee!" shouted Dizzy Dave.

"Look what I've got, Henry," said Greedy Graham, holding a bulging bag of sweets.

"Gimme some," said Henry.

"And me," said Rude Ralph.

The three boys stuffed their faces with sweets.

"Ugh, a green lime," said Henry, taking the sticky sweet out of his mouth. "Eeech." He flicked the sweet away.

PING!

The sweet landed on Moody Margaret's neck.

"Ow," said Margaret.

She turned round and glared at Henry.

"Stop it, Henry!" she snarled.

"I didn't do anything," said Henry.

PING!

A sweet landed in Sour Susan's hair.

PING!

A sweet stuck on Anxious Andrew's new jumper.

"Henry's throwing sweets!" shouted Margaret.

Miss Battle-Axe turned round.

"Henry! Sit next to me," she said.

"I needed a wee!" wailed Weepy William.

Finally, the bus drove up to the Frosty Freeze Factory. A gigantic, delicious-looking ice cream cone loomed above it.

"We're here!" shouted Henry.

"You scream! I scream! We all scream for ice cream!" shrieked the children as the bus stopped outside the gate.

"Why are we waiting here?" yelled Greedy Graham. "I want my ice creams now!"

Henry stuck his head out of the window. The gates were chained shut. A large sign read: "CLOSED on Mondays."

Miss Battle-Axe looked pale. "I don't believe this," she muttered.

"Class, there's been a mix-up, and we seem to have come on the wrong day," said Miss Battle-Axe. "But never mind. We'll go to –"

"The Science Museum!" shouted
Clever Clare.

"The zoo!" shouted Dizzy Dave.

"Lazer Zap!" shouted Horrid
Henry.

"No," said Miss Battle-Axe. "Our
Town Museum."

"Ugggghhhhh," groaned the class.

No one groaned louder than
Horrid Henry.

The children left their jackets and
lunch boxes in the packed lunch room,
and then followed the museum guide
to Room 1.

"First we'll see Mr Jones's
collection of rubber bands," said the
guide. "Then our famous display of
door hinges and dog collars through
history. And don't worry, you'll be

seeing our latest acquisitions, soil
from Miss Montague's garden and
the Mayor's baby pictures."

Horrid Henry had to escape.

"I need a wee," said Henry.

"Hurry up then," said Miss
Battle-Axe. "And come straight
back."

The toilets were next to the packed
lunch room.

Henry thought he'd make sure his
lunch was still there. Yup, there it
was, right next to Ralph's.

I wonder what Ralph has got,
thought Henry, staring at Ralph's
packed lunch. No harm in looking.

WOW. Rude Ralph's lunch box
was bursting with crisps, sweets, and
a chocolate spread sandwich on white
bread.

He'll feel sick if he eats all that junk

food, thought Henry. I'd better help him.

It was the work of a moment to swap Ralph's sandwich for Henry's egg and cress.

This certainly isn't very healthy, thought Henry, gazing at Greedy Graham's goodies. I'll do him a favour and exchange a few of my celery sticks for his sweets.

43

Just look at all those treats, thought Henry, fingering Sour Susan's cakes. She should eat a more balanced meal.

A pack of raisins zipped from Henry's lunch box to Susan's and a sticky bun leapt from Susan's to Henry's.

Tsk tsk, thought Henry, helping himself to Tough Toby's chocolate bar and replacing it with an apple. Too many sweets are bad for the teeth.

44

That's better, he thought, gazing at his re-packed lunch with satisfaction. Then he strolled back to his class, who were gathered round a glass case.

"This is the soil in which Miss Montague grew her prize-winning vegetables," droned the guide. "She grew marrows, tomatoes, potatoes, leeks —"

"When do we eat?" interrupted Horrid Henry.

"I'm starving," whined Greedy Graham.

"My tummy's rumbling," groaned Rude Ralph.

"When's lunch?" moaned Moody Margaret.

"WE'RE HUNGRY!" wailed the children.

"All right," said Miss Battle-Axe. "We'll eat now."

The class stampeded down the hall and grabbed their lunches. Henry sat in a corner and tucked in.

For a moment there was silence, then the room echoed with howls of dismay.

"Where's my sticky bun?" yelped Sour Susan.

"My sweets are gone!" screamed Greedy Graham.

"What's this? Egg and cress? Yuck!" shouted Rude Ralph, hurling the sandwich at Anxious Andrew.

That did it. The room filled with flying carrot and celery sticks, granola bars, raisins, crusts, and apples. Henry smirked as he wiped the last traces of chocolate from his mouth.

"Stop it! Stop it!" howled Miss Battle-Axe. "Well done, Henry, for being the only sensible child. You may lead us back to see the pieces of Roman pottery in Room 2."

Horrid Henry walked proudly at the head of the shuffling, whining children. Then he noticed the lift at the far end. A sign read:

STAFF ONLY:
DO NOT ENTER

I wonder where that lift goes, thought Horrid Henry.

"Stop him!" yelled a guard.

But it was too late.

Henry had dashed to the lift and pressed the top button.

Up up up he zipped.

Henry found himself in a small room filled with half-finished exhibits. On display were lists of overdue library books, "lightbulbs from 1965 to today," and rows and rows of rocks.

Then, in the corner, Henry actually saw something interesting: a dog's skeleton protected by a drooping blue cord.

Henry looked more closely.

It's just a pile of bones, thought Henry.

He wobbled the blue cord then stood on it.

"Look at me, I'm a tight-rope walker," chortled Horrid Henry, swaying on the blue cord. "I'm the best tight-rope walker in – AGGGHHHH!"

Horrid Henry lost his balance and toppled against the skeleton.

CLITTER-CLATTER! The bones crashed to the ground.

DING DING DING. A burglar alarm began to wail.

Museum guards ran into the room.

Uh-oh, thought Horrid Henry. He slipped between a guard's legs and ran. Behind him he could hear pounding feet.

Henry dashed into a large room filled with road signs, used bus tickets and traffic cones. At the other end of the room Henry saw Peter's class gathered in front of "The Story of the Drain". Oh no. There was Mum.

Henry ducked behind the traffic cones.

Museum guards entered.

"There he is!" shouted one. "The boy in the purple T-shirt with the gold stars."

Henry stood fixed to the spot. He was trapped. Then the guards ran straight past his hiding place. A long arm reached over and plucked Perfect Peter from his group.

"Come with us, you!" snarled the
guard. "We're going straight to the
Bad Children's Room."

"But . . . but . . ." gasped Peter.

"No ifs or buts!" snapped the
guard. "Who's in charge of this
child?"

"I am," said Mum. "What's the
meaning of this?"

"You come too," ordered the
guard.

"But . . . but . . ." gasped Mum.

52

Shouting and protesting, Mum and Perfect Peter were taken away.

Then Henry heard a familiar booming voice.

"Margaret, that's enough pushing," said Miss Battle-Axe. "No touching, Ralph. Stop weeping, William. Hurry up, everyone! The bus leaves in five minutes. Walk quietly to the exit."

Everyone immediately started running.

Horrid Henry waited until most of the children had charged past then re-joined the group.

"Where have you been, Henry?" snapped Miss Battle-Axe.

"Just enjoying this brilliant museum," said Horrid Henry. "When can we come back?"

3

HORRID HENRY
AND THE
DEMON DINNER LADY

"You're not having a packed lunch and that's final," yelled Dad.

"It's not fair!" yelled Horrid Henry. "Everyone in my class has a packed lunch."

"N–O spells no," said Dad. "It's too much work. And you never eat what I pack for you."

"But I hate school dinners!" screamed Henry. "I'm being poisoned!" He clutched his throat. "Dessert today was— bleeeach—fruit salad! And it had worms in it! I can feel them slithering in my stomach

– uggghh!" Horrid Henry fell to the
floor, gasping and rasping.

Mum continued watching TV.

Dad continued watching TV.

"I love school dinners," said Perfect
Peter. "They're so nutritious and
delicious. Especially those lovely spinach
salads."

"Shut up, Peter!" snarled Henry.

"Muuuum!" wailed Peter. "Henry told
me to shut up!"

"Don't be horrid, Henry!" said Mum.
"You're not having a packed lunch and
that's that."

Horrid Henry and his parents had been fighting about packed lunches for weeks. Henry was desperate to have a packed lunch. Actually, he was desperate *not* to have a school dinner.

Horrid Henry hated school dinners. The stinky smell. The terrible way Sloppy Sally ladled the food *splat!* on his tray so that most of it splashed all over him. And the food! Queueing for hours for revolting ravioli and squashed tomatoes. The lumpy custard. The blobby mashed potatoes. Horrid Henry could not bear it any longer.

"Oh please," said Henry. "I'll make the packed lunch myself." Wouldn't that be great! He'd fill his lunchbox with four packs of crisps, chocolate, doughnuts, cake, lollies, and one grape. Now that's what I call a real lunch, thought Henry.

Mum sighed.

Dad sighed.

They looked at each other.

"If you promise that everything in your lunchbox will get eaten, then I'll do a packed lunch for you," said Dad.

"Oh thank you thank you thank you!" said Horrid Henry. "Everything will get eaten, I promise." Just not by me, he thought gleefully. Packed lunch room, here I come. Food fights, food swaps, food fun at last. Yippee!

Horrid Henry strolled into the packed lunch room. He was King Henry the

Horrible, surveying his unruly subjects.
All around him children were screaming
and shouting, pushing and shoving,
throwing food and trading treats. Heaven!
Horrid Henry smiled happily and opened
his Terminator Gladiator lunchbox.

Hmmn. An egg salad sandwich. On
brown bread. With crusts. Yuck! But he
could always swap it for one of Greedy
Graham's stack of chocolate spread
sandwiches. Or one of Rude Ralph's jam

rolls. That was the great thing about packed lunches, thought Henry. Someone always wanted what you had. No one *ever* wanted someone else's school dinner. Henry shuddered.

But those bad days were behind him, part of the dim and distant past. A horror story to tell his grandchildren. Henry could see it now. A row of horrified toddlers, screaming and crying while he told terrifying tales of stringy stew and soggy semolina.

Now, what else? Henry's fingers closed on something round. An apple. Great, thought Henry, he could use it for target practice, and the carrots would be perfect for poking Gorgeous Gurinder when she wasn't looking.

Henry dug deeper. What was buried right at the bottom? What was hidden under the celery sticks and the granola bar? Oh boy! Crisps! Henry loved crisps. So salty! So crunchy! So yummy! His mean, horrible parents only let him have crisps once a week. Crisps! What bliss! He could taste their delicious saltiness already. He wouldn't share them with anyone, no matter how hard they begged. Henry tore open the bag and reached in—

Suddenly a huge shadow fell over him. A fat greasy hand shot out. Snatch! Crunch. Crunch.

Horrid Henry's crisps were gone.

Henry was so shocked that for a moment he could not speak. "Wha—wha—what was that?" gasped Henry as a gigantic woman waddled between the tables. "She just stole my crisps!"

"That," said Rude Ralph grimly, "was Greta. 'She's the demon dinner lady.'"

"Watch out for her!" squealed Sour Susan.

"She's the sneakiest snatcher in school," wailed Weepy William.

What? A dinner lady who snatched food instead of dumping it on your plate? How could this be? Henry stared as Greasy Greta patrolled up and down the aisles. Her piggy eyes darted from side to side. She ignored Aerobic Al's carrots. She ignored Tidy Ted's yoghurt. She ignored Goody-Goody Gordon's orange.

Then suddenly—

Snatch! Chomp. Chomp.
Sour Susan's sweets were gone.
Snatch! Chomp. Chomp.
Dizzy Dave's doughnut was
gone.

Snatch! Chomp.
Chomp. Beefy Bert's
biscuits were gone.
Moody Margaret
looked up from her
lunch.

"Don't look up!" shrieked Susan. Too
late! Greasy Greta swept Margaret's food
away, stuffing Margaret's uneaten
chocolate bar into her fat wobbly cheeks.

"Hey, I wasn't finished!" screamed
Margaret. Greasy Greta ignored her and
marched on. Weepy William tried to hide
his toffees under his cheese sandwich. But
Greasy Greta wasn't fooled.

Snatch! Gobble. Gobble. The toffees

vanished down Greta's gaping gob.

"Waaah," wailed William. "I want my toffees!"

"No sweets in school," barked Greasy
Greta. She marched up and down, up and
down, snatching and grabbing, looting
and devouring, wobbling and gobbling.

Why had no one told him there was a
demon dinner lady in charge of the
packed lunch room?

"Why didn't you warn me about her,
Ralph?" demanded Henry.

Rude Ralph shrugged. "It wouldn't
have done any good. She is unstoppable."

We'll see about that, thought Henry.
He glared at Greta. No way would
Greasy Greta grab his food again.

On Tuesday Greta snatched Henry's
doughnut.

On Wednesday Greta snatched Henry's
cake.

On Thursday Greta snatched Henry's
biscuits.

On Friday, as usual, Horrid Henry persuaded Anxious Andrew to swap his crisps for Henry's granola bar. He persuaded Kung-Fu Kate to swap her chocolates for Henry's raisins. He persuaded Beefy Bert to swap his biscuits for Henry's carrots. But what was the use of being a brilliant food trader, thought Henry miserably, if Greasy Greta just swooped and snaffled his hard-won treats?

Henry tried hiding his desserts. He tried eating his desserts secretly. He tried tugging them back. But it was no use.

The moment he snapped open his lunch box – SNATCH! Greasy Greta grabbed the goodies.

Something had to be done.

"Mum," complained Henry, "there's a demon dinner lady at school snatching our sweets."

"That's nice, Henry," said Mum, reading her newspaper.

"Dad," complained Henry, "there's a demon dinner lady at school snatching our sweets."

"Good," said Dad. "You eat too many sweets."

"We're not allowed to bring sweets to school, Henry," said Perfect Peter.

"But it's not fair!" squealed Henry. "She takes crisps, too."

"If you don't like it, go back to school dinners," said Dad.

"No!" howled Henry. "I hate school dinners!" Watery gravy with bits. Lumpy surprise with lumps. Gristly glop with

globules. Food with its own life slopping about on his tray. NO! Horrid Henry couldn't face it. He'd fought so hard for a packed lunch. Even a packed lunch like the one Dad made, fortified with eight essential minerals and vitamins, was better than going back to school dinners.

He could, of course, just eat healthy foods. Greta never snatched those. Henry imagined his lunchbox, groaning with alfalfa sprouts on wholemeal brown bread studded with chewy bits. Ugh! Bleeeach! Torture!

He had to keep his packed lunch. But he had to stop Greta. He just had to.

And then suddenly Henry had a brilliant, spectacular idea. It was so brilliant that for a moment he could hardly believe he'd thought of it. Oh boy, Greta, thought Henry gleefully, are you going to be sorry you messed with me.

Lunchtime. Horrid Henry sat with his lunchbox unopened. Rude Ralph was armed and ready beside him. Now, where was Greta?

Thump. Thump. Thump. The floor shook as the demon dinner lady started her food patrol. Horrid Henry waited

until she was almost behind him. SNAP! He opened his lunchbox.

SNATCH! The familiar greasy hand shot out, grabbed Henry's biscuits and shovelled them into her mouth. Her terrible teeth began to chomp.

And then——-

"Yiaowwww! Aaaarrrgh!" A terrible scream echoed through the packed lunch room.

Greasy Greta turned purple. Then pink. Then bright red.

"Yiaowwww!" she howled. "I need to cool down! Gimme that!" she screeched, snatching Rude Ralph's doughnut and stuffing it in her mouth.

"Aaaarrrgh!" she choked. "I'm on fire! Water! Water!"

She grabbed a pitcher of water, poured it on top of herself, then ran howling down the aisle and out the door.

For a moment there was silence. Then the entire packed lunch room started clapping and cheering.

"Wow, Henry," said Greedy Graham, "what did you do to her?"

"Nothing," said Horrid Henry. "She just tried my special recipe. Hot chilli powder biscuits, anyone?"

4

HORRID HENRY'S SPORTS DAY

"We all want sports day to be a great success tomorrow," announced Miss Battle-Axe. "I am here to make sure that *no one*" – she glared at Horrid Henry – "spoils it."

Horrid Henry glared back. Horrid Henry hated sports day. Last year he hadn't won a single event. He'd dropped his egg in the egg-and-spoon race, tripped over Rude Ralph in the three-legged race, and collided with Sour Susan in the sack race. Henry's team had even lost the tug-of-war. Most sickening of all, Perfect Peter had won *both* his races.

If only the school had a sensible day,

like TV-watching day, or chocolate-eating day, or who could guzzle the most crisps day, Horrid Henry would be sure to win every prize. But no. *He* had to leap and dash about getting hot and bothered in front of stupid parents. When he became king he'd make teachers run all the races then behead the winners. King Henry the Horrible grinned happily.

"Pay attention, Henry!" barked Miss Battle-Axe. "What did I just say?"

Henry had no idea. "Sports day is cancelled?" he suggested hopefully.

Miss Battle-Axe fixed him with her steely eyes. "I said no one is to bring any sweets tomorrow. You'll all be given a delicious, refreshing piece of orange."

Henry slumped in his chair, scowling. All he could do was hope for rain.

Sports day dawned bright and sunny. Rats, thought Henry. He could, of course, pretend to be sick. But he'd tried that last year and Mum hadn't been fooled. The year before that he'd complained he'd hurt his leg. Unfortunately Dad then caught him dancing on the table.

It was no use. He'd just have to take part. If only he could win a race!

Perfect Peter bounced into his room.

"Sports day today!" beamed Peter. "And *I'm* responsible for bringing the hard-boiled eggs for the egg-and-spoon races. Isn't it exciting!"

"NO!" screeched Henry. "Get out of here!"

"But I only …" began Peter.

Henry leapt at him, roaring. He was a cowboy lassoing a runaway steer.

"Eeeaaargh!" squealed Peter.

"Stop being horrid, Henry!" shouted Dad. "Or no pocket money this week!"

Henry let Peter go.

"It's so unfair," he muttered, picking up his clothes from the floor and putting

them on. Why did he never win?

Henry reached under his bed and
filled his pockets from the secret sweet
tin he kept there. Horrid Henry was a
master at eating sweets in school without
being detected. At least he could scoff
something good while the others were
stuck eating dried-up old orange pieces.

Then he stomped downstairs. Perfect
Peter was busy packing hard-boiled eggs
into a carton.

Horrid Henry sat down scowling and
gobbled his breakfast.

"Good luck, boys," said Mum. "I'll be there to cheer for you."

"Humph," growled Henry.

"Thanks, Mum," said Peter. "I expect I'll win my egg-and-spoon race again but of course it doesn't matter if I don't. It's *how* you play that counts."

"Shut up, Peter!" snarled Henry. Egg-and-spoon! Egg-and-spoon! If Henry heard that disgusting phrase once more he would start frothing at the mouth.

"Mum! Henry told me to shut up," wailed Peter, "and he attacked me this morning."

"Stop being horrid, Henry," said Mum. "Peter, come with me and we'll comb your hair. I want you to look your best when you win that trophy again."

Henry's blood boiled. He felt like snatching those eggs and hurling them against the wall.

Then Henry had a wonderful, spectac-

ular idea. It was so wonderful that …
Henry heard Mum coming back down
the stairs. There was no time to lose
crowing about his brilliance.

Horrid Henry ran to the fridge,
grabbed another egg carton and swapped
it for the box of hard-boiled ones on the
counter.

"Don't forget your eggs, Peter," said
Mum. She handed the carton to Peter,
who tucked it safely in his school bag.

Tee hee, thought Horrid Henry.

Henry's class lined up on the playing
fields. Flash! A small figure wearing
gleaming white trainers zipped by. It was
Aerobic Al, the fastest boy in Henry's class.

"Gotta run, gotta run, gotta run," he
chanted, gliding into place beside Henry.
"I will, of course, win every event," he
announced. "I've been training all year.

My dad's got a special place all ready for my trophies."

"Who wants to race anyway?" sneered Horrid Henry, sneaking a yummy gummy fuzzball into his mouth.

"Now, teams for the three-legged race," barked Miss Battle-Axe into her megaphone. "This is a race showing how well you co-operate and use teamwork with your partner. Ralph will race with

William, Josh will race with Clare, Henry
…" she glanced at her list, "… you will
race with Margaret."

"NO!" screamed Horrid Henry.

"NO!" screamed Moody Margaret.

"Yes," said Miss Battle-Axe.

"But I want to be with Susan," said
Margaret.

"No fussing," said Miss Battle-Axe.
"Bert, where's your partner?"

"I dunno," said Beefy Bert.

Henry and Margaret stood as far apart
as possible while their legs were tied
together.

"You'd better do as I say, Henry,"
hissed Margaret. "*I'll* decide how we
race."

"*I* will, you mean," hissed Henry.

"Ready … steady … GO!"

Miss Battle-Axe blew her whistle.

They were off! Henry moved to the
left, Margaret moved to the right.

"This way, Henry!" shouted Margaret. She tried to drag him.

"No, this way!" shouted Henry. He tried to drag her.

They lurched wildly, left and right, then toppled over.

CRASH! Aerobic Al and Lazy Linda tripped over the screaming Henry and Margaret.

SMASH! Rude Ralph and Weepy William fell over Al and Linda.

BUMP! Dizzy Dave and Beefy Bert collided with Ralph and William.

"Waaa!" wailed Weepy William.

"It's all your fault, Margaret!" shouted Henry, pulling her hair.

"No, yours," shouted Margaret, pulling his harder.

Miss Battle-Axe blew her whistle frantically.

"Stop! Stop!" she ordered. "Henry! Margaret! What an example to set for the younger ones. Any more nonsense like that and you'll be severely punished. Everyone, get ready for the egg-and-spoon race!"

This was it! The moment Henry had been waiting for.

The children lined up in their teams. Moody Margaret, Sour Susan and Anxious Andrew were going first in

Henry's class. Henry glanced at Peter. Yes, there he was, smiling proudly, next to Goody-Goody Gordon, Spotless Sam, and Tidy Ted. The eggs lay still on their spoons. Horrid Henry held his breath.

"Ready ... steady ... GO!" shouted Miss Battle-Axe.

They were off!

"Go Peter go!" shouted Mum.

Peter walked faster and faster and faster.

He was in the lead. He was pulling away
from the field. Then … wobble … wobble
… SPLAT!

"Aaaaagh!" yelped Peter.

Moody Margaret's egg wobbled.

SPLAT!

Then Susan's.

SPLAT!

Then everybody's.

SPLAT!

SPLAT!

SPLAT!

"I've got egg on my shoes!' wailed Margaret.

"I've ruined my new dress!" shrieked Susan.

"I've got egg all over me!" squealed Tidy Ted.

"Help!" squeaked Perfect Peter. Egg dripped down his trousers.

Parents surged forward, screaming and waving handkerchiefs and towels.

Rude Ralph and Horrid Henry shrieked with laughter.

Miss Battle-Axe blew her whistle.

"Who brought the eggs?" asked Miss Battle-Axe. Her voice was like ice.

"I did," said Perfect Peter. "But I brought hard-boiled ones."

"OUT!" shouted Miss Battle-Axe. "Out of the games!"

"But … but …" gasped Perfect Peter.

"No buts, out!" she glared. "Go straight to the Head."

Perfect Peter burst into tears and crept away.

Horrid Henry could hardly contain himself. This was the best sports day he'd ever been to.

"The rest of you, stop laughing at once. Parents, get back to your seats! Time for the next race!" ordered Miss Battle-Axe.

All things considered, thought Horrid Henry, lining up with his class, it hadn't been too terrible a day. He'd loved the egg-and-spoon race, of course. And he'd had fun pulling the other team into a muddy puddle in the tug-of-war, knocking over the obstacles in the obstacle race, and crashing into Aerobic Al in the sack race. But, oh, to actually win something!

There was just one race left before sports day was over. The cross-country run. The event Henry hated more than

any other. One long, sweaty, exhausting
lap round the whole field.

Henry heaved his heavy bones to the
starting line. His final chance to win …
yet he knew there was no hope. If he
beat Weepy William he'd be doing well.

Suddenly Henry had a wonderful,
spectacular idea. Why had he never
thought of this before? Truly, he was a
genius. Wasn't there some ancient Greek
who'd won a race by throwing down

golden apples which his rival kept stopping to pick up? Couldn't he, Henry, learn something from those old Greeks?

"Ready … steady … GO!" shrieked Miss Battle-Axe.

Off they dashed.

"Go, Al, go!" yelled his father.

"Get a move on, Margaret!" shrieked her mother.

"Go Ralph!" cheered his father.

"Do your best, Henry," said Mum.

Horrid Henry reached into his pocket and hurled some sweets. They thudded to the ground in front of the runners.

"Look, sweets!" shouted Henry.

Al checked behind him. He was well in the lead. He paused and scooped up one sweet, and then another. He glanced behind again, then started unwrapping the yummy gummy fuzzball.

"Sweets!" yelped Greedy Graham. He stopped to pick up as many as he could

find then stuffed them in his mouth.

"Yummy!" screamed Graham.

"Sweets! Where?" chanted the others. Then they stopped to look.

"Over there!" yelled Henry, throwing another handful. The racers paused to pounce on the treats.

While the others munched and crunched, Henry made a frantic dash for the lead.

He was out in front! Henry's legs moved as they had never moved before, pounding round the field. And there was the finishing line!

THUD! THUD! THUD! Henry glanced back. Oh no! Aerobic Al was catching up!

Henry felt in his pocket. He had one giant gob-stopper left. He looked round, panting.

"Go home and take a nap, Henry!" shouted Al, sticking out his tongue as he raced past.

Henry threw down the gob-stopper in front of Al. Aerobic Al hesitated, then skidded to a halt and picked it up. He could beat Henry any day so why not show off a bit?

Suddenly Henry sprinted past. Aerobic Al dashed after him. Harder and harder, faster and faster Henry ran. He was a bird. He was a plane. He flew across the finishing line.

"The winner is … Henry?" squeaked

Miss Battle-Axe.

"I've been robbed!" screamed Aerobic Al.

"Hurray!" yelled Henry.

Wow, what a great day, thought Horrid Henry, proudly carrying home his trophy. Al's dad shouting at Miss Battle-Axe and Mum. Miss Battle-Axe and Mum shouting back. Peter sent off in disgrace. And he, Henry, the big winner.

"I can't think how you got those eggs muddled up," said Mum.

"Me neither," said Perfect Peter, sniffling.

"Never mind, Peter," said Henry brightly. "It's not winning, it's *how* you play that counts."